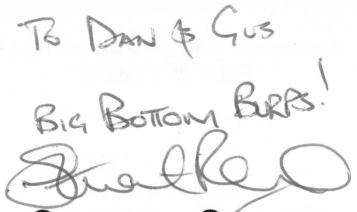

To Dan & Gus

Big Bottom Burps!

Gorgeous George

And his Stinky, Stupid Stories

By

Stuart Reid

Illustrations, Cover and Layouts
By John Pender

CONTENTS

Holy Flying Cows, Buttman!
A Grandpa Jock short story

The hot desert air blew warmth against the soldier's face, specks of sand pebble-dashing his cheeks. The breeze rippled through his huge, ginger moustache as his eyes focused hard on the panicking creature.

Just beyond the ridge a brown cow rose up off the ground, bathed in a green glow of light. The animal bellowed wildly in distress as it rose higher and higher into the sky; the brilliant beam drawing the creature into a shadow of blackness. Stars blanketed the clear June sky, sweeping east to west, apart from that one large spot of pure darkness directly above. Was it a spaceship? The soldier couldn't be sure.

'Dang it, I told ya's. There goes another one,' moaned a scruffily-dressed rancher lying on the rocky outcrop beside the soldier. The hillbilly lifted his right buttock off the ground and ripped out a long, rasping blast. The desert air became warmer and mustier. The soldier didn't flinch, staring into the sky.

By now, the cow was further above their heads, still kicking and braying, bathed in a luminous lime-green cone, and the soldier's eyes never left the floating animal. Just as the bovine reached the peak, the light changed. Green flashed purple, then nothing. Blackness. The two men blinked furiously, still blinded by the beam of light, even though it was no longer there. The night sky seemed darker than ever.

'So how long do we wait now?' asked the soldier, scanning the skies again as his eyes adjusted to the night.

'S'pose it'll be 'bout an hour,' huffed the rancher. He rolled onto his back and stared into the night. 'Lord only knows where they go or what's being done to them but you can bet your butt they'll be back.'

'How long have you been witnessing these… happenings, Mr Chiggins?'

'You can call me Pete,' he drawled lazily. 'Or Pongo. Or Pongo Pete. Ev'body else does.'

The rancher turned to the soldier now, his tattered blue dungarees dusty with sand. The night was warm yet Pongo wore a thick checked shirt and heavy boots; his dirty pink vest was popping out from under his collar. Large damp patches had formed under his arm-pits many times, dried then dampened again. He lifted his leg and another ripper cut ominously through the night. 'Pongo' was an appropriate name.

'Well, I've been living out in this ol' desert for near on fifty years, an' I aint' seen nothin' like this before.' Pongo rolled the wad of chewing tobacco around to his other cheek.

'But since the start of '47 things have changed. These last few months have been weird.' Pongo spat into the sand. 'My cattle's been hornswoggled by sum'thing up there and nobody's taken me serious since. That was why I was so glad when you showed up, Major.'

Pongo stared across at the soldier. The major was dressed in black combat pants, black storm-breaker jacket and a tooled-up black webbing belt. There was a pistol strapped against his thigh and a pair of binoculars were hung across the front of his chest. Reality was beginning to hit the old rancher now, and as relieved as he was that his complaints were being listened to, he knew nothing about the soldier lying beside him.

'And you ain't from round these parts, soldier, so how in the name of Socksmudgin' Sam did you ever find out about this stuff? You ain't regular army, are you?'

The major smiled, shook his head and pulled off his black beret to reveal a receding hairline in front of a thick crop

2

of fiery red hair. He looked at his watch, then across to the large field radio that lay alongside, its antenna reaching 10 feet into the sky. The radio sat on a large, padlocked trunk.

'Sir, I haven't been entirely honest with you.'

The major spoke with a heavy Scottish accent and the ginger bristles of his big moustache rippled as he spoke. His dark eyes were serious but there was a hint of humour there.

'Yes, I am Major Jock Hansen, and I am with the military…' he paused. 'Just not with the American military. I represent a covert operation called the Black Ops Order of British Intelligence & Espionage Services.'

Major Jock Hansen hesitated for a second, watching the rancher as the little cogs whirred furiously around in his head. It hadn't sunk in yet but he was slowly getting there.

'Yes, sir,' interrupted Hansen, 'I work for BOOBIES.' The major let Pongo process the information quickly, then he began again…

'For the last two years, the Black Ops team has been working all around the globe gathering intelligence in countries that we believe do not have the capabilities to manage that information for themselves.' The major stopped again waiting for the rancher to catch up.

'But this is America, son.' Pongo still couldn't see the connection.

'Exactly, sir,' Hansen went on. 'Since the end of the Second World War, we've been monitoring a highly classified situation here in New Mexico. Your cow abductions are just the tip of the iceberg.'

'You mean you guys knew about this,' exclaimed Pongo. He'd met with a wall of disbelieving silence since he first reported his disappearing cattle, as the police, the state troopers and even the army had refused to believe the ramblings of a senile old rancher with bowel problems.

3

Most of them were just glad to get him out of their office.

Just then static crackled and the radio burst into life.

'Boobies calling Buttman. Boobies calling Buttman. Come in Buttman.'

'Your code name is Buttman?' sniggered the old rancher, lifting his leg again to pass more intestinal gas.

Major Jock smiled again. 'Yes, sir. We've been monitoring you too, sir. Buttman just seemed er… appropriate.'
He picked up the radio and carried on.

'This is Buttman here. Go ahead. Over.'

'We have detected aerial activity in your location, Buttman. Can you confirm? Over'

'That's an affirmative. Activity confirmed but unspecified. Over.'

Major Jock released the button on the side of the chunky transmitter. Pongo stared across at him, his eyes half closed. He struggled hard to understand the Scottish accent. Words like 'affirmative' only sound good with an American twang.

'Message received and understood. Standby for incoming. Boobies over and out.'

Lightning crackled overhead. The once clear dark sky was beginning to ripple with thunder clouds and the stars were soon blocked out. Thick mist rolled across the night sky, filled with occasional flashes; electricity sparkling and energy bursting intensely. Was that a shadow moving within the cloud.

Major Jock put the radio to one side and patted the wooden trunk.

'Best of British, sir. It's show time!'

Down in the valley the herd moved slowly to the west. Hundreds of cattle, with deep red, almost mahogany hides were meandering gently across the river, soft bellows echoing into the night. In their plodding memories, the evening's earlier panic was slowly fading into oblivion. Chewing the cud was priority again and they grazed gracefully, occasionally lifting their heads but generally munching on tufts of wild grass.

But even to the most casual of observers there may have been something slightly amiss down on the desert floor. Most of the animals were moving west. Most of the cattle were dark brown in colour. Most of the cows didn't swear when they tripped.

Only one animal was stumbling away from the herd, heading east, back onto the wide open prairie. Alone. Unprotected by the safety of the group. The animal staggered awkwardly over the uneven ground, cursing wildly.

Oddly, this creature had rather distinctive markings, large patches of black splashed on white. And if our casual observer was aware of the differences in cattle breeds, they would've known that this Holstein-Friesian breed was renowned, and bred, for its high yield dairy production, whereas the Red Angus was commonly used in beef production.

In fact, if our observer was more cattle connoisseur than casual spectator, then they would have known of the tale of Grey-Breasted Jock, considered the Grandfather of the Breed and given the No.1 Pedigree in The Scottish Herd Book, and the cow Old Granny, born in 1824, lived to 35 years of age and produced 29 calves. More Angus cattle trace their roots back to her than any other single cow of the breed.

But it didn't take an expert to notice that this black and white animal was a different breed altogether. The back end moved independently from the front. The front end swore in a guttural Scottish accent, whilst the rear cursed like a dang hillbilly. The hide of the animal was threadbare and patchy, and looking closely, it might be possible to see the butt-end of a dusty pair of dungarees through the moth-eaten holes in the costume.

And cows don't usually wear boots!

Now truly alone in the prairie, the black and white cow made a tempting target for the predators of the night. Too far from the rest of the herd; small, isolated, unbalanced and…

A piercing beam of brilliant light burst onto the desert floor, illuminating the unique animal. The cow's head snapped back, startled, and its feet began to rise up off the ground. The green glow, with its pulsating energy, pulled the cow into the sky and into the belly of the black shadow above.

'Dumfungled cattle rustlers!' cursed the cow's bottom.

'Dagnabbit! Are you sure you know what the heck you're doing, son?' The rancher had been swearing since his feet had left the prairie.

Major Jock laughed again, stepping out of his black and white mottled trousers.

'Best of British, I told you,' grinned the major. 'Pantomime cows have been used in Britain for years, and we're in here now, aren't we?'

'Sure but…' the rancher paused, looking around. 'Where's here?'

Pongo and Major Jock glanced about as they discarded

the rest of their cow costume. The white patches on the hide shone dazzling white, whilst the black cloth seemed to melt into the background. The walls hummed with a light purple glow.

They stood in a small, circular cell with a hexagonal seal below their feet, and beneath the underside of a deep purple dome above their heads. The dome was covered in tiny pyramids, each pyramid part of a group of four; little isosceles edges, divided into larger equilateral triangles. Major Jock reached up and touched it. Ripples of purple and blue shimmered across the surface.

'Class 2 Frequency 16 Icosahedrons,' said Major Jock casually. 'Basically, we're underneath the base of a geodesic sphere... a power ball.'

'Looks like a bug's eye,' muttered Pongo. 'Like a fly or sum'thing.'

Major Jock was now examining the floor. 'The cattle would be pulled in through these six triangular doors in the floor...' He was talking aloud to himself, more than to the rancher. 'Using some kind of gravitational tractor beam, and powered by the sphere.'

'Light source is an electromagnetic pulse wave, vibrating on frequencies higher than we can identify; ultra-violet, if you like,' he went on. 'These frequencies are invisible to humans, but visible to insects. It's a non-ionising radiation which can produce up to 10% of the energy of sunlight.'

'So... are we in some kinda spaceship?' gulped Pongo Pete, still trying to understand his environment.

'Yes, sir. And this will be the top secret technology of the future, if we can capture any of it, sir,' and Major Jock began running his hands across the surface of the walls. Pongo's face was pale, and it shone brightly in the violet hue. He gulped again, and without moving emitted another large gaseous parp.

This seemed to trigger sensors in the dome above, as it began to crackle. Before Major Jock could reply a doorway rose in the curved wall in front of them, revealing darkness beyond. Sparks of electricity shot down from the ceiling and zapped into the bodies of the two men, pushing them towards the black doorway.

'Aaargh, dagnabbit!' grunted Pongo, hopping towards the doorway and holding onto his sizzling butt. Major Jock led the way, not to evade the painful lasers but because he was intrigued to find out what lay ahead.

On the other side of the short, narrow corridor was a metal holding pen, surrounded on three sides with steel bars and a high ceiling above. As Pongo staggered into the pen he saw that Major Jock had already climbed up the fence and was sitting on top, like a rodeo cowboy on the bars.

'Come on, up here, quickly,' ushered the major and he offered his hand down to the startled rancher. They grabbed tightly together and Jock pulled him up to safety. No sooner had Pongo reached the safety of the top spar that the doorway sealed off behind them and a pile of green pellets were dumped into a trough at the front of the cage. An enormous tin-foil bag then dropped down from the darkness above. Coils and wires were attached to the bag and long rubber straps folded themselves around each other at the bottom of the pen.

Major Jock looked up and stared around the vastness. Above and behind them was an enormous, throbbing globe. It reached high into the air and curved away around to the side. Surrounding the dome were thousands of pens, forming concentric circles moving outward and upward from the centre. The cages were slowly revolving around the dome.

In most of the pens stood a silent, wide-eyed cow, each

attached to the inflatable silver bags. In their comatose state the animals munched blindly, chewing down food pellets, in unconscious suspension.

'Absolute genius!' breathed Major Jock. Pongo stared around him as he watched the foil bags slowly began to swell.

'I beg your pardon,' he droned, almost as bewildered as the cattle surround him.

'Genius, I said,' gasped the ginger-haired soldier. He pointed back down to the doorway.

'We were drawn into the holding cell and you set off the sensors when they detected your… er… methane gas. Thinking we were another animal, the automated system 'encouraged' us forward with electric shocks into this production pen.'

'Like a cattle prod,' Pongo mumbled slowly. A new reality was dawning on the old rancher, as he became aware that his understanding of the world and the whole universe was changing forever.

'Exactly,' exclaimed Major Jock. 'The cattle are pushed in here and those rubber straps are programmed to tie around the hind quarters of each cow. The animals are fed compressed, green fodder pellets, probably rich is protein, causing bacterial fermentation to take place in one of a cow's four stomach compartments. Digestive flatulence will then occur… into the silver bags.'

'You mean to say those balloons are filling up with cow farts!' exclaimed Pongo, rubbing his nose with his hand.

'Yes sir,' replied Major Jock. 'Volatile fatty acids are created when the animal eats food, then regurgitates it, chews the cud and swallows it again. This digestion produces a massive amount of methane, ammonia and nitrogen. The aliens must be using those chemicals to power their crafts.'

'Did you… did you just say 'aliens'?' Another piece of the jigsaw fell into place in Pongo's new universe.

'Who else built this baby, sir?' grinned Major Jock. 'But don't worry; we're not planning to meet up with them just yet. This was only a sightseeing trip.'

'But we might be meeting the little critters sooner than you think,' squealed the rancher, pointing back down to where they'd come in. The doorway was shooting upwards, revealing two feet with three toes each and a short pair of legs, clad in tight-fitting, metallic outfit.

'I hope so, sir. That's how I was planning to leave.'

Before the door could fully open, Major Jock had leapt forward and jumped onto the silver foil bag, swinging towards the opening. He stretched his feet out and struck something full in the face, if you could call it a face. They both went down in a heap and Major Jock performed a perfect combat roll to land on his haunches like a cat.

'I was hoping they would check on their faulty bovine. No gas, you see.' The major pointed to the bag, which had been torn down in the action. 'Let's go!'

The cattle farmer gawped at the soldier, who was clearly enjoying himself, as the major pulled a little box from the belt of the unconscious being lying on the floor.

Major Jock picked up the foil bag and grabbed Pongo's shirt, pulling him towards the corridor. Only then did Pongo have a chance to turn and look back into the pen. The creature on the floor was short, just over a metre tall, with a strange humanoid appearance. Its flight-suit was black and its enlarged head was a dull blue colour. Pongo couldn't make out the eyes but there were two tiny spots of black where the nose should be and a thin slit for a mouth.

Just before he was hauled out of sight by the marauding major, Pongo would swear later he saw the large opaque, black eyes blink furiously. But not blinking, as such, more like blankets of skin pulsating from within the eyes themselves.

Major Jock charged back to the circular cell and flashed the little box across almost indiscernible panel in the wall. Steam hissed, and the hexagonal doors in the floor opened outwards. Daylight was beginning to break through above the clouds and the ultraviolet shade of the cell merged into a white-blue.

'Have you ever parachuted before?' said Major Jock, raising his eyebrow with a twinkle. 'This would be a good day to learn.'

Major Jock clipped the rubber cables onto his black webbing belt. He pulled old Pongo in close, extended a thick strap around his waist and gasped. The old rancher was sweating again and the build-up under his arms was over-powering. The major took a deep breath and stepped through the hole in the floor.

At that moment, two more images were emblazoned into Pongo's brain. First, the sight of their pantomime cow costume, both sets of legs, the body and the ludicrously large head had begun to dissolve against the wall. The black and white fur was sizzling and melting away; grey fluffy run-off dribbling towards trap door.

Next, those penetrating black eyes appeared around the corner. As the blue-skinned alien stepped out of the violet shade and into the pale daylight its skin became an almost translucent grey colour. The eyes remained dark and wide, and Pongo felt an energy burn into every recess of his brain. His every thought and memory and dream, in every corner of his mind was purged and clawed over. He felt violated. He passed gas. He passed out.

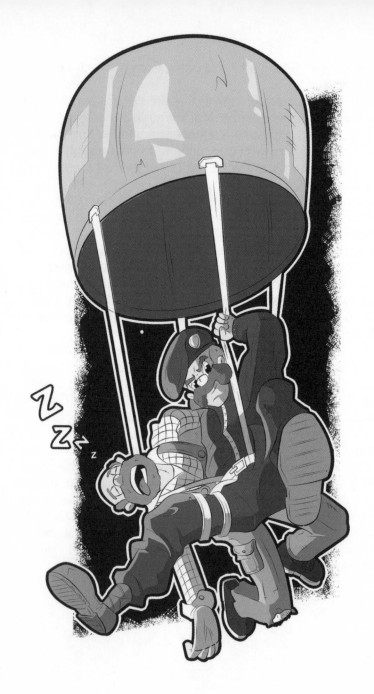

When he woke, Pongo was firmly back down on terra firma. Major Jock, the man in black, was furiously packing away his field radio and other equipment; clearly, the silver foil bag had doubled a parachute. Away in the distance a small plume of dust was approaching. Pongo searched the skies but saw nothing but blistering sunshine.

'Where did they go?' demanded the rancher. 'The spaceship was there a moment ago.'

'I'm sorry, sir, I'm not sure I know what you're referring to,' replied the major as dry and monotone as possible. 'And I need to go before the real army gets here. It's going take some explaining.'

'But you saw it. You were there!' shouted the rancher and he tugged at the major's shoulder. As he spun him round, Pongo stepped back, shocked. The major's face was burned red and beginning to blister.

'UV light and sunshine's no good for us gingers,' said Major Jock, winking at the cattle farmer. 'But it'll make one hell of a story to tell our grandkids, won't it?!'

Unfortunately for Pongo Pete, Major Jock Hansen disappeared almost into thin air, and the old cattleman was left with some explaining to do and a lot more puzzled faces were looking for answers. Pongo thought it best to gloss over the part about BOOBIES or Buttman but he couldn't really explain the silver foil bag that had been his parachute.

Shortly after his interrogation, the military police simply let him go, warning him to keep his mouth shut. Apparently, there had been a crash and the officers' attention was called elsewhere.

The following day, the Roswell Army Air Field released a press statement announcing their operations group had recovered a "flying disk", which had crashed on a ranch near Roswell. The story sparked intense media interest across the globe.

Almost as soon as the story hit the headlines, the Commander General of the US Eighth Air Force convened a press conference to declare it was actually a weather balloon that had been recovered by the RAAF personnel. A slightly embarrassed air force officer was forced to kneel in front of photographers showing off the alleged debris from the crashed object.

Of course, the silver foil balloon was thinner and more pliable than anything the pressmen had ever seen before, whilst the straps and cables were stronger that steel but the Commander General declared,

'That's the technology of the future, gentlemen. And it's top secret.'

The End

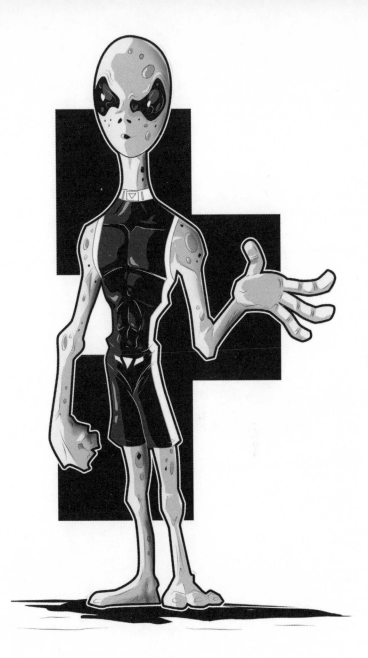

Three Little Monkeys

Not last night
But the night before,
Three little monkeys
Came to my door

One with a trumpet,
One with a drum,
And one with a pancake stuck up his bum!

Allison Thunderpants
An Allison short story

Allison was beginning to get very tired of sitting beside her two friends, Gorgeous George and Crayon Kenny, and of having nothing to do. Once or twice she peeped into the book the boys were reading, but it was just pictures of animals doing silly things, 'and what use is a book' thought Allison 'without words or conversation.'

So she was considering in her own mind (as well as she could, for the hot day had made her feel very sleepy) whether the pleasure of making a daisy-chain would be worth the trouble of getting up and picking the daisies, when suddenly a Green Rabbit with pink eyes ran close by her.

There was nothing so very remarkable about that; nor did Allison think is very unusual to hear the Rabbit say to itself 'Oh dear! Oh dear! I'm late. I'm late!' but when the Rabbit actually took a smart-phone out from within the folds of its nappy, and looked at it and hurried on, Allison started to think it was slightly strange. She had never seen a green rabbit before, nor a rabbit that wore a nappy either, and she was certain that rabbits didn't, or couldn't use smart-phones; they had no opposable thumbs, for a start.

Burning with curiosity, Allison ran across the field after it, just in time to see it pop down a large rabbit-hole under a hedge. She dived in, never once considering how she was going to get out.

The rabbit-hole dipped suddenly down and before she knew it she found herself falling down a very deep well.

Either the well was very deep, or she was falling very slowly, for she had plenty of time to look around her. She was falling passed cupboards and book shelves, and noticed they were full of bottles and jars filled with coloured smoke. She took one down, an orange one; it was labelled 'Baked Beans,' but she was disappointed that the jar contained nothing but orange cloudy puffs. She put it back in a hurry.

'I wonder if I'll fall straight through the centre of the earth,' thought Allison. 'Maybe I'll come out in India or Thailand. They make lovely, spicy food in Thailand, don't they?'

Down, down, down. Would her fall never come to an end! There was nothing else to do, so Allison began to talk to herself. Do only mad people talk to themselves? Grandpa Jock talks to himself all the time and George's grandfather is as mad as they come but he's good fun, and he says he always gets the right reply.

'Grandpa Jock will miss me very much tonight,' she said. 'I hope he remembers to add coconut cream to his curry this evening, just to tone it down a little. The last time he thought his bottom had exploded. Pebble-dashed the porcelain, he said.'

And here Allison began to feel rather sleepy, and went on saying to herself 'Pebbledash the porcelain. Pebbledash the porcelain. Pebbledash the porcelain.' The more often she said it, the more the words sounded like a very runny poo splattering in a toilet but of course, Allison was a polite young lady, and her mother would never approve of such thoughts.

Then suddenly, thump! She came down upon a green velvet cushion, with little puffs of dust billowing gently up into the air, and the fall was over.

Allison was not hurt a bit, and as she jumped to her feet, the cushion melted softly into the emerald-coloured carpet. She had no time to consider how weird it all was because before her was a long passage, and the Green Rabbit was still hurrying down it. Allison ran after the odd little bunny and could just hear it saying to itself 'I'm only green thanks to the Queen. How angry will she be if I'm late?!'

Allison was sure she was close behind it when she turned the corner, but the Rabbit was no longer to be seen; instead she saw a small door, like a cat-flap, or indeed, a rabbit-flap, set into a brick wall near the floor. She was much too big to fit through there, she thought, and anyway, shouldn't cat-flaps be fitted in doors, not walls?

Then Allison turned and saw a little three-legged table (she was certain it hadn't been there before) and on top of the table was a small, red bottle of Tabasco sauce. Around the neck of the bottle was a label, with the words 'Drink Me' printed on it.

'It was all very well to say "Drink me,"' thought Allison, and she had seen Grandpa Jock slurp spicy sauce for a dare but she had heard stories about children burning their bums by splashing Tabasco sauce on their food.

'But then again, it doesn't actually say poison,' pondered Allison. She ventured to taste some, almost certain that the fiery red liquid would disagree with her at some time. No sooner had her lips touched the bottle when she began glugging back the hot sauce. She couldn't stop herself; it was as if the bottle was glued to her lips and she slugged it back furiously.

Only when she'd drained the last of its contents did the bottle finally release itself from her mouth. Allison gasped in a lungful of air and the sharp pepper taste scratched at the back of her throat.

'What a curious feeling!' said Allison, and she began to feel her tummy tremble. Her knees were knocking and she felt like a giant bubble was bouncing around inside her. Suddenly the bubble dropped like a stone, hot and heavy, thumping down deep in the pit of her stomach.

She lurched forward.

Her belly gurgled. Allison clutched her tummy. Her belly

gurgled again, lower this time. Allison clutched her bottom. But she was too late.

Allison's arse exploded! The bang was deafening enough but the shockwave in such a confined space pulverised the wall, the table and the cat-flap. Bricks flew in every direction, splinters of wood were shot through the air and smoke billowed around the corridor.

Only… there was no corridor. Had she blown it away? She was standing in a beautiful garden, surrounded by beds of bright flowers, trailing willow trees and cool fountains. There was a sundial in the centre of the lawn, and on it lay a large red chilli. Tied to the green stalk of the pepper was a paper label with the words 'Eat Me' neatly printed on it.

'I'm not falling for that again,' snapped Allison haughtily and turned on her heels. 'One bum blast is enough for any day.'

And just as she turned she heard the tiny pattering of little feet. It was the Green Rabbit again, its fur was still green, perhaps it had been white at some point but now it was fluffier than ever, as if it had been for a spin in a tumble drier.

'Wait!' shouted Allison but the Rabbit didn't stop. It ran right passed her, hopped over a flower bed and ducked behind a willow tree. Allison gave chase.

The air was cooler in the shade and one tree led to another, and another, and another. The trailing leaves became thicker and the light grew darker. Allison stepped around another tree and a glade opened up around her. Again the Rabbit was nowhere to be seen but there, lurking in the shadows, were two enormously fat little boys. They were wearing red and white striped trousers, red jackets and little paper hats on their heads. Each wore a gold name badge pinned onto their chest.

Allison stared hard. She couldn't tell them apart, the boys

were identical. The only difference she could see was that the first name badge read 'Poodlebum' and the other read 'Poodlepee.'

'Curiouser and curiouser!' whispered Allison to herself and the boys giggled.

'Do you find something amusing?' asked Allison politely, but there was a slight edge to her voice. The twins began whispering, bowing their heads together and nodding feverishly. Then they clasped their podgy hands to their mouths and sniggered.

'I'm not sure what you think is so funny,' she declared. The boys giggled to themselves again; their shoulders wobbled, sending ripples across their tummies.

'I mean, I'm not the one named after a dog's bottom,' announced Allison looking at the twin on the left. The boys stopped laughing. 'Nor one named after a dog's wee-wee,' she said, turning to the boy on her right. Their faces began to blaze brightly and their piggy little eyes glared. Without warning, they burst into song.

'I'm Poodlebum,'

'I'm Poodlepee,'

'Can we take your order, please?'

'Spicy bean burgers are all that's left,'

'But we'll give you extra cheese.'

Allison stared in amazement. After the boys stopped singing two of the largest fake smiles Allison had ever seen spread across their faces.

'You're running a fast food restaurant?' gasped Allison. 'At the bottom of someone's garden?' The boys looked at each other and started to sing again.

'It's the only job… that we could find.'

'And we like taking orders.'

'The Queen pays twenty pence an hour',

'But we eat all her burgers.'

23

'Yes, I can see that,' said Allison, nodding at their bulging waistbands. 'Maybe you chaps should think about cutting back a little.'

'We only eat bean burgers. We don't care about our diet.'

'We like the wind it gives us. Come on, you should try it!'

'Erm, no,' replied Allison, looking at the boys suspiciously. 'No, I don't think I will.'

'All this wind…' said Poodlebum, 'For twenty pence an hour.'

'Where would we be…' said Poodlepee, 'without our pump parp power.'

Just then, the lad on the left lifted his right leg. In a mirror image, the boy on the right lifted his left leg and the two of them simultaneously let out a pair of long, rasping bottom burps. In stereo!

Allison was sure she felt the ground tremble and she pulled her head back slightly, trying to distance herself from the bilging cloud of obnoxious fumes. The boys had certainly been overdosing on their own products and had built up quite a gas reserve between them. No longer embarrassed, the twins grinned wildly at Allison, and she choked as the smell caught her at the back of the throat.

'The time has come…' said Poodlebum, 'To talk of many beans.'

'Of shoes and shocks…' said Poodlepee, 'Of cabbages and queens.'

Both boys lifted their legs again, but before they could dump another colonic explosion, Allison turned away and the earth shook again. A giant, black shadow of stench flew behind her and she ran deeper into the trees. In the distance she heard the boys laughing merrily to themselves.

Allison ran and ran and ran. The trees grew thicker, the darkness grew blacker and Allison became hopelessly lost. When she eventually stopped running, Allison flopped down

against a stump and breathed deeply. At least the air here was fresh and clean, and as she gasped, her chin slumped down upon her chest.

It was at that moment she heard a polite cough above her head. She looked up sharply and saw an impossibly tartan cat looking down at her with large round eyes, sitting in the bough of a tree.

Allison was a little startled at first but as she looked closer she realised that the creature had the body of a cat and the head of an balding old man; receding on top, yet with a huge fringe of bushy ginger whiskers.

The cat-man's tail flicked casually back and forth, and occasionally a paw would swipe lazily at butterflies as they fluttered passed. Its body was a mixture of orange, white and black stripes, indeed tiger stripes but not in the conventional, up-and-down-direction that tiger stripes normally follow. These stripes were horizontal, vertical and even diagonal and Allison could only think of one word for them – tartan. Who'd ever heard of a tartan cat?

Beneath the bushy ginger moustache on the cat-man's top lip, Allison was sure that it was smiling at her. It looked good natured, she thought: still it had very long claws and a great many teeth, although they did look false, she still felt that it ought to be treated with respect.

'Ginger-Jock,' she began, rather timidly, not sure at all whether such a name was suitable for a tartan, half-man, half-cat; however it only grinned a little wider and Allison felt enough confidence to go on.

'Please, would you tell me which way I should go from here?' she asked.

'That depends a good deal on where you want to go to,' said the cat-man.

'Poodlebum and Poodlepee,' she remarked, 'mentioned a Queen. The Green Rabbit did too. Perhaps she could help me find my way home.'

'Visit the Queen?' Ginger-Jock sat up. 'Visit the Queen? Are you mad? You must be mad to come here.'

'Why would I be mad to visit the Queen' replied Allison.

'Because the Queen is mad,' Ginger-Jock went on, its tail pointing off down the path. 'And you must be mad to want to go and see her. And I must be mad to be telling you. We're all mad!'

And with a small squeaky pump, Ginger-Jock, the tartan cat-man, vanished quite slowly, beginning with the end of the tail and ending with its bushy moustache, which remained some time after the rest of it had gone.

Allison waited a little, half expecting to see it again, but it did not appear, and after a minute or two she walked on in the direction in which the Queen was said to live.

She had not gone much further along the path before her nostrils began to twitch. The atmosphere became stale, and every breath was hot and fetid. As the trees began to thin out, the air started to thicken with the pungent odour of cabbage soup and Allison was sure there was a green shimmer to every breeze.

And then, Allison found herself at last in another beautiful garden with a cool flowing fountain in the very centre, among brightly coloured blossoms and rows upon rows of green beans. A large chilli bush stood near the entrance, its fruit glowing rich red and vibrant. As Allison walked passed it she noticed that the entire garden was filled with chilli plants and beans; hundreds upon hundreds of them.

Next to the fountain stood a very grand woman, red and regal, her face crimson to the point of exploding. Allison wasn't sure if she was angry or just sunburnt. She was glaring down at the ground and it was then that Allison noticed the Green Rabbit running around her feet. He kept picking chillies and dropping them into a pestle, as the Queen shouted 'More, more, more!'

'Yes, your Majesty. At once, your Majesty,' muttered the little bunny as it scurried around madly in its over-sized nappy, pulling the chillies off the bushes and occasionally throwing a few green beans in the pot for good measure.

Once the granite bowl was overflowing with chillies and beans, the Green Rabbit began banging away with a heavy stone pestle, grinding the vegetables into a thick mushy paste. The Queen could contain her impatience no longer and she pushed the Rabbit out of the way and began scooping her bare hands around the bowl and shovelling the spicy mixture into her mouth. Her face began to glow even redder, if that was at all possible.

Mouthful followed spicy mouthful of the Rabbit's chilli bean paste until the sludge was finished and the Queen began licking each of her fingers clean, taking care to nibble out the gunge from under every fingernail. All the time the Rabbit hopped back and forth, singing…

'Queen's beans. Scoff them up fast.'

'The more you eat, the more you'll blast.'

Allison had been watching intently for a few minutes but as soon as she took one step forward into the garden the Queen turned immediately, her gaze catching Allison full in the face.

'Who is this?' screamed the monarch in a loud, shrill voice. The Green Rabbit instantly jumped up and began bowing furiously.

'Idiot!' screamed the Queen, tossing her head back impatiently and the Rabbit trembled at the sound of her voice.

'My name is Allison, if it pleases your Majesty,' said Allison very politely; but she added, to herself, 'Why, it's still Allison, even if it doesn't please your Majesty.' Luckily, the Queen didn't hear her.

'And why are you in the Royal Chilli Garden? No one sets foot in the Royal Chilli Garden without my permission!' she shrieked.

'How should I know?' said Allison, surprised at her own courage. 'I fell down a rabbit-hole and I've been trying to find my way home ever since.'

'Rabbit-hole! Rabbit-hole!' yelled the Queen. For a moment her face turned from crimson to purple with fury, and, after glowering at Allison for moment, she screeched 'I've never heard such insolence. Off with her--'

'Nonsense!' said Allison, very loudly and decidedly, and the Queen was silent. She stood, like a ticking time-bomb, anger simmering a fraction below the surface.

'How dare you address me in such a manner, insolent child!' The Queen was glaring at her. 'No one speaks like that to the Queen of Farts.'

'The Queen of Farts?' giggled Allison, realising how ridiculous it sounded but the Green Rabbit hopped over to her quickly and peered anxiously into her face.

'Hush! Hush!' said the Rabbit in a low, hurried tone. It looked anxiously over his shoulder as he spoke, and then raised himself up on tiptoe, put his mouth close to her ear and whispered 'Please don't upset her now.'

'Upset her?' replied Allison. 'I would never dream of upsetting anyone.'

'That's her third bowl of chilli beans and the Queen is ready to blow....' the Rabbit began.

Allison gave a little scream of laughter. 'Oh hush!' the Rabbit whispered in a frightened tone. 'She's already late, you see, and who has to clean up the mess? I do, that's who.'

'Get to your places!' shouted the Queen in a voice of

29

thunder, and the terrified Rabbit began running in all directions, pulling dozens of glass jars from underneath hedgerows. The jars were all different shapes and sizes but all of them had fixed lids and rubber seals around the stoppers.

'Quickly!' squealed the Rabbit. 'There's not much time. Help me, please.'

Allison thought she had never seen such a curious sight in all her life. The Green Rabbit had collected a large pile of jars in the centre of the garden; the Queen was now bent over with her dress pulled up around her waist and her bare bottom was pointing towards the fountain. The Rabbit was gripping onto one of the larger jars, ready to catch whatever the Queen was about to fire out.

At first it was a low rumble but soon the Queen's wind built up into a deafening, thunderous explosion. The poor Rabbit held on tightly to its glass jar until suddenly he snapped the lid shut and picked up another. Allison saw that the first jar contained a green gas.

'It's green,' remarked Allison.

'Of course it's green. Haven't you seen my fur this week,' replied the Rabbit. 'Sometimes it's orange, some weeks it's baked beans, sometimes it's yellow when all she eats are eggs, and other times, well, you wouldn't really want to know. Just help me with another jar.'

Allison picked up a medium sized jar this time and handed it to the Rabbit, who was trying his utmost to fill each container with the Royal wind.

'No, you catch some too.' And the Rabbit pushed the jar back into Allison's hands.

The chief difficulty Allison found at first was the power with which the Queen blasted out of her bottom. Allison thought that the Queen of Farts was not a title that had been gained easily and she almost lost her footing on several occasions but held on tightly to each jar until every one was filled with cloudy smoke.

Allison was becoming quite tired by all her efforts when she noticed that the wind was slowing and the Queen was beginning to strain even harder. Beside her, Allison noted, the Rabbit was trembling more than ever.

It was at that moment that the Queen's royal behind erupted and spewed forth an enormous torrent of watery poo. All the plants in the garden were covered as the spray splattered everywhere and the Queen let out a little squeal. Pebbledashtheporcelain, pebbledashtheporcelain…

As soon as the very last squirt of poo-juice plopped out the Queen picked up the frightened Rabbit and began to wipe her bottom with the furry little animal. The Rabbit's eyes were closed tightly as he was shaken up and down and the green gunk clogged up his hair.

When she was done wiping the Queen tossed the Rabbit into the nearest chilli patch and almost before the Rabbit hit the ground he had shaken off his nappy and bolted for the gate. Allison stared in amazement. The top half of the Rabbit was thick and matted in green poo whilst the bottom half, the part protected by the nappy, was still white and fluffy.

The Queen then plonked her bottom down into the fountain and great jets of steam rose up from the water. A look of magisterial relief spread across the Queen's face and Allison could have sworn there were tears in her eyes.

Allison began looking around for some way to escape, and wondering if she could get away without being seen when she noticed a curious appearance in the air; it puzzled her at first but after watching for a second or two, she made out a fiery orange moustache, and she said to herself 'It's the Ginger-Jock.'

'How are you getting on?' said the cat-man, as soon as the rest of the head appeared.

'I don't think it's very fair at all,' Allison began, in rather a complaining tone. 'That poor Rabbit used to be white and now it's all green and…and mucky… and….'

'How do you like the Queen?' said the cat-man in a low voice.

'Not at all,' replied Allison. 'She's so extremely…'

Just then she noticed the Queen had lifted her bottom out of the fountain and was looking intently across at her.

'Who are you talking to?' roared the Queen, waving her hand towards the head of the Ginger-Jock.

'It's a friend of mine… a Ginger-Jock,' said Allison. 'Allow me to introduce him.'

'It looks rather fluffy,' said the Queen of Farts. 'However, it may kiss my bottom if it likes.'

'I'd rather not,' the cat-man remarked as his ginger whiskers began to disappear quickly again.

'Don't be impertinent,' said the Queen, 'and don't look at me like that!'

'There's just a moustache left,' declared Allison. 'I'm sure that's the only way he can look.'

'Hold your tongue!' bellowed the Queen, turning purple again.

'I won't!' said Allison.

'Off with her head!' The Queen of Farts shouted at the top of her voice but there was nobody there to carry out her orders. The Green-but-used-to-be-White Rabbit had scurried off to safety (and hopefully, to have a shower) and the Ginger-Jock had disappeared completely. The chilli garden was empty, still and silent... except for…

Allison strained her ears; she began to hear giggling. She closed her eyes tightly and could definitely hear the sound of laughter echoing out from beyond; the snickering of two small boys. She opened her eyes.

'Wake up, stinky!' laughed Gorgeous George. 'You've got

a bum like a bull.'

'Oh, I've had such a curious dream,' said Allison, still taking a moment to awaken.

'Yeah, and you've been pumping all the time you were sleeping,' chuckled Crayon Kenny, picking his nose with long stalk of grass. 'We've been practically choking here.'

'I don't know what you had for your lunch,' sniggered George. 'But your butt is honking. Have you been eating Grandpa Jock's curries again?'

'Eggy cabbage?' suggested Kenny with a grin.

'Red hot chilli beans?' laughed George.

Allison smiled and closed her eyes again.

Lastly, Allison pictured herself a grown woman, and how she would keep, through all her riper years, the warm, lovable wind of her childhood, and how she would find pleasure in simple child-like jars of joys and happy summer days.

The End

Full acknowledgment is given to Lewis Carroll, as a tribute to his work Alice in Wonderland – the most fantastical piece of children's nonsense ever written.

Beans!

Beans, beans,
The musical fruit.

The more you eat,
The more you toot!

Beans, beans,
They're good for your heart.

The more you eat,
The more you fart!

Lovesick Lion and the Valentine Vomit
A Gorgeous George short story.

First Chapter

'Bleeeeeeuugghhhhhhhh!'

George heard the sickening noise retching through the downstairs bathroom window as he approached the house. Inside, someone was barfing.

'Beeeeeeuuuuuuuuugggggggggggghhhhhhhhh! Bleugh, bleugh.........blah.'

There was a sigh of relief, and then some breathless panting. A small throat was cleared, rasping up whatever yucky stuff was still hanging around, and that was quickly followed by an inexperienced, dribbly spit. George could imagine the trails of saliva dangling down and he shook his head and hurried passed the window, as a delicate voice chirped,

'That's it, that's it, sweetie. Bring it all up... hock it all out now. That's it.'

George ran to the front door and rung the bell. Instantly the door flew opened and a wild-haired boy jumped out with his jacket over his arm. He grabbed George by the elbow and dragged him away from the house, as more puking noises echoed from the bathroom.

'Run, Gorgeous,' choked Kenny. 'It's a like a sea of sick in there.' And the two boys sprinted down the garden path, across the road and kept running until they'd reached the grassy knoll at the bottom of the park. They sat down on the stump of a fallen tree and gasped for breath.

Gorgeous George, as you've probably guessed, wasn't all that gorgeous. Even in the best light, George could only be described as 'interesting'. His head was an ever-so-slightly-odd shape, his mouth turned down at one side, just a tiny bit and his ears stuck out. His Grandpa Jock always said that body parts grow at different times and his head was just waiting for the rest of his face to catch up.

Crayon Kenny, on the other hand, was one of the most unpredictably chaotic boys George had ever met. On his day he could be described as slightly eccentric; on any other day, and usually the ones with a 'Y' in them, Kenny would be classed as stark raving bonkers. He had developed the unusual hobby of sticking crayons, marbles, macaroni and just about anything else up his nose, just to see what it felt like. This talent started when he was much younger and now he'd honed it to perfection. And as they sat there on the tree stump, Kenny absent-mindedly scratched away at the inside of his nostril with a small twig.

'Was that your little brother I heard?' asked George, politely. 'The one barfing up the entire contents of his stomach in the bathroom?'

'Oh yeah, sorry George,' replied Kenny. 'You weren't meant to hear that but my mum had to open the window because of the smell.'

'It was a bit…. ripe,' yakked George, 'even outside. I caught a whiff as I walked passed, it was honking! What had the booger-brain been eating?'

'Mum says she's not sure if it's a tummy bug or not but you know Johnny, the little freak'll eat anything. He was sick in his bedroom first thing this morning. It was on the carpet, it was all over his bed. George, it was even up the walls.'

George stuck his tongue out of the corner of his mouth and pretended to barf, then covered it with his hand, laughing.

'I'm not kidding, George. He just sat there, in his bed, spewing projectile vomit all over the place, whilst my mum ran around with a basin trying to catch each gobful.'

'I suppose when you're little, you're never quite sure when

puke is going to creep up on you.'

'HE'S FIVE!' yelled Kenny. 'He should know better by now, he's been sick before. We all know once the watery bit starts, we've got about 10 seconds to stick our heads down the toilet… at least make it to the sink. But, oh no, perfect little Johnny just sits there… chucking up carrots and sweetcorn and goodness knows what else all over the place. George, I can't remember the last time we even had sweetcorn!'

'Okay, okay. Calm down, mate,' chuckled George. 'You've had a bit of a shock this morning.'

Although it seemed funny, George thought it was more than just shock, his friend seemed quite traumatised by the whole episode. And that was saying something, about the boy who had been known to snort an entire plateful of baked beans up his nose in the canteen, then swallow them down the back of his throat. True, the beans hadn't shot back up again, along with the rest of his stomach contents but as school stunts go, it was pretty gross. George tried to take his mind off it.

'Did I tell you my grandpa's got a new girlfriend?' said George, as casually as it's possible to drop any bombshell.

'WHAT?' shrieked Kenny, his mind instantly distracted from the thought of his little brother swimming around in a pool of puke. 'Your grandpa? Mr Jock? The baldy old geezer in the kilt? But, but, but… he's ancient!' Kenny paused, slowly allowing the thought sink into his brain. He shuddered.

'What do mean a "new girlfriend", George? I didn't even know he had an old one.'

'Well, this one is fairly old, she must be at least seventy, so Mum says. I haven't met her yet but Mum says she's got white hair and false teeth and everything.'

'What's an old duffer like your grandpa doing getting

himself a girlfriend? No offence, mate.'

George shrugged. 'I dunno, he says it keeps him young but I hardly see him these days. He's always up the town, she's got a shop there.'

No one was quite sure how old Grandpa Jock was exactly, even he said he stopped counting at the turn of the century. That is to say, the turn of the 20th century into the 21st century. Grandpa Jock might've been alive in the 19th century, nobody was too sure but that would've made him really, really old but since he'd given up wearing suits and ties, and turned his back on being smart and sensible and mature, he'd found a new zest for life.

'She's owns a shop?' asked Kenny with a raised eyebrow, a new thought slowly seeping into his head. 'What kind of shop?'

'I'm not too sure. My grandpa hasn't said.'

'Maybe she's a fishmonger?' suggested Kenny.

'Ooh no, she'd stink. I hope she just smells like old people.'

'What? You mean, she'll smell of wee!' laughed Kenny.

'Old people don't smell of wee… not all of them. My Grandpa Jock doesn't smell like that,' argued George.

'Yeah but that's because he wears a kilt. If he was a normal old man, and he dribbled when he was at the toilet, his trousers would smell of wee. Makes sense, doesn't it?' Kenny turned up his nose and wiggled his fingers in disgust.

'Aw man, too much information, dude,' groaned George. 'And anyway, if she sold fish I would've caught a whiff. I was standing quite close to her.'

'Ooh George, what if she runs a sweet shop?!' Kenny's eyes were lighting up. 'Maybe she sells sweets and chocolate and little jelly worms and toffees and ice cream.' Kenny was practically drooling now. 'And maybe she needs two young lads to work as special sweetie testers, you know, to try out new products… or just to get rid of some old products, the stuff that isn't selling and she needs to make space on the shelves for new ones. Or… or… or maybe she sells cakes. Old ladies are great at baking cakes and…'

'Calm down, Kenny, man. I don't know what kind of shop she's got.' George dug around in one of his pockets. 'My grandpa wrote the address down, here it is.' George pulled out a slip of paper.

Number 54, Fungus Road, the note read.

'We should go down there, you know, right now.' Kenny was still secretly hoping Grandpa Jock's new girlfriend's shop would involve some confectionary tasting and maybe he'd get to lick the spoon, or even the bowl or maybe….

'HOLD IT!' shouted Kenny at the top of his voice. He was suddenly aware that his mind had been racing ahead and his brain was three steps further down the road than his mouth. George turned and stared at him.

'It's too good to be true, George,' said Kenny, with a look of repulsed horror on his face. 'What if we get down there, right, and this woman and your Grandpa Jock are, well, you know…' Kenny paused. 'Kissing!'

'Aw no, man! That's just wrong,' yelled George, putting his fingers in his ears.

'But they might be,' Kenny went on. 'They're boyfriend and girlfriend…'

'I'm not listening.' George had screwed up his eyes to block out the words.

'And we go in and they're all smoochy, smoochy… and we're, like,…'

'Lalalalalalalalalalalalalalalalalalalalalalalalalalalalala!' sang George, sticking his fingers in his ears, desperately trying to stop a whole range of horrible thoughts entering his head.

'And they're kissing so hard that their false teeth come out and they're all gumsy, and slobbering over each other like two slobbery big Labradors.' Kenny now pushed his lips out like a fish and started making kissy, kissy noises in George's ear, whilst George went into denial and curled himself into a ball.

'Myah, myah, myah, Monsieur Jock,' pretended Kenny. 'Give me a big kissy.'

'Er… what's going on here?' came a voice from the other side of a tree. Kenny jumped off George and the two boys tried to see who was coming.

'That's rather strange behaviour, don't you think?' The girl was smirking at the boys as she walked round to join them on the big log.

'Uh, it's only Allison,' breathed Kenny with a sigh of relief. Allison was a smart girl, very sensible and grown up for her age, so she never understood why she liked hanging around with a couple of numbskulls like George and Kenny. Sure, they made her laugh, of course they'd been on loads of adventures together and George's Grandpa Jock was one of the most entertaining old people she'd ever met but, boy, could they be thick sometimes.

'I thought I'd find you two here,' she smiled pleasantly. 'What were you doing?'

'Mr Jock has got himself a new girlfriend,' Kenny blurted out, keen to share the news. 'And she's got a sweet shop, or a bakery or something, and I was just pretending to be them, all cute and yucky and stuff.'

'Aw, that's lovely,' said Allison.

'LOVELY?!' cried both the boys together.

'It's disgusting!' said Kenny.

'They're ancient,' added George.

'Yes, I know,' replied Allison. 'But everyone's entitled to a little love, whatever age they are. I think it's nice they've found each other.'

'What is love anyway?' asked George, his face still screwed up in a nauseated grimace.

'Love,' began Allison, and George wished he hadn't asked the question. 'is when two people feel warm and fuzzy about each other, and they enjoy each other's company, and chatting to one another, and they like holding hands.'

'Mushy stuff then,' replied George.

'No one is sure why it happens,' Kenny butted in. 'But I heard it has something to do with how you smell. That's why perfume and deodorant are so popular.'

'But you said that Grandpa Jock's girlfriend might smell like wee or even fish,' giggled George. 'My grandpa's not going to fancy a lady if she smells of fish.'

'Yeah but she might smell of cakes and chocolate.' Kenny was drooling again. 'Even I'd fancy a girl if she smelled like chocolate.'

'Well, boys, it's Valentine's Day tomorrow so I'm delighted Mr Jock has found someone to share it with. He's been on his own for a long time, George.' Allison nodded wisely, but George was loathe to admit she had a point. It was still all yucky stuff to him.

'Have they been out on a date yet, George?' sniggered Kenny, hiding his face behind his hands. George glared at him.

'I hope not,' George spat. 'What a waste of money! People go out on dates all romantic and stuff, and they end up staring at each other until their food gets cold.'

'Not all the time, George. Dates are about having fun, and getting to know each other,' Allison went on. 'Even boys have something interesting to say if you listen long enough.'

George and Kenny stopped and looked at each other. Kenny stuck two fingers down his throat and pretended to gag. 'Bleugh,' he barfed.

'Right, you two, that's enough,' announced Allison, and

the boys knew that their nonsense was finished. 'Why don't we go into town and meet this lady? I'm sure she's very nice and we'll probably bump into Mr Jock too.'

Kenny continued being pretend sick but George just shrugged his shoulders. He hadn't seen his grandpa for a couple of days and this old dear was hogging all his attention, so maybe it was a good idea to meet her head on. And of course Kenny might be right, there may be sweets involved.

Decision made, Allison jumped up and marched off towards the main road into town, leaving the boys to follow her at a trot.

Middle Chapter

Now George, Allison and Kenny all lived in the small town of Little Pumpington, and Fungus Road was in the very centre of town. It wasn't called Fungus Road because it was filled with mushrooms and little patches of blue mould growing everywhere - that's Mildew Lane, don't get confused.

No, Fungus Road was so called after Little Pumpington's second mayor, the honourable Frederick Fungus, who won the right to become mayor when he defeated the original title-holder, Bartholomew 'Smokey' Bamshot in a duel for the Mayorship over two hundred years ago. Nobody really knows how the duel was fought, as it was held in secret deep in the woods but there's a rumour it involved lots of Brussel sprouts and rotten cabbages.

Anyway, you're not here for a history lesson; you want to learn about love.

Allison turned down into Fungus Road and stopped at the corner. She counted along the numbers above all the shops until she came to number 54. The sign above the door read.

'Paws and Claws.'

'There's Mr Jock there, inside the shop.' Allison was pointing through the glass, beyond the display of cute fluffy kittens in the window, to a spot at the back of the shop, next to the till. George and Kenny pressed in close to Allison so they could see what was going on too.

Grandpa Jock was standing smiling, holding a large bunch of flowers and a red card. The lady opposite was beaming back, her eyes twinkling with delight. She was a small bird-like woman with a kind face and a nest of golden hair at the back of her head. She wore half-moon glasses on the end of her nose and she was staring intently at Grandpa Jock.

'Urgh, she owns a pet shop,' groaned Kenny, realising he wasn't going to taste any free cakes, chocolates or sweets today.

'She looks lovely,' simpered Allison. 'Just like a proper Nana.'

'She looks like a banana?' screeched George. 'I don't want my Grandpa Jock dating a banana. She might get eaten.'

Kenny smiled and joined in. 'If they went to the cinema on a date and Mr Jock got hungry, he could eat one of her arms. Cinema prices are really expensive for hot dogs and popcorn.'

Allison rolled her eyes. 'Not a banana! Nana, like 'Gran' or 'Granny'. Have you never heard of a Nana before?'

Of course we have, we're just joking. George barely heard the words echoing in his head. Kenny might've spoken but George couldn't have been sure, he wasn't listening. He was too busy staring towards the couple at the counter.

Now George could be a thoughtful lad, when he wasn't thinking about bottom burps and bogies, and sometimes he liked to watch people, to think about what was going through their minds. Occasionally people would say things they didn't really mean, but they've give it away with a

45

twitch, or a glance. It was amazing to George how much he could glean from a look, or a snort, or a faked laugh. There was another language, hidden behind words, that used tones, glances and tiny movements of the face that the owners were never aware of. People who thought their faces were completely blank did not realise how much they were broadcasting of their innermost thoughts, to anyone smart enough to spot the signs.

To George, Grandpa Jock's signs were flashing in bright neon letters high above his head, blinking hypnotically, like Piccadilly Circus. And strangely, the little pet-shop lady's body language was saying the same sort of things back. George felt a little uneasy and Allison noticed.

'It's alright, George,' she said, putting her hand on his arm. 'Don't be jealous. Old people need love too.' And George sighed and felt his heart soften, knowing Allison was right and there was more than enough of Grandpa Jock to go around.

'Aw man!' yelled Kenny, pointing in the window. 'She's trying to steal his chewing gum now!'

Inside the shop Grandpa Jock and the pet-shop lady were kissing, and she was running her hand through the patch of ginger hair around the side of his head (there was definitely no hair on top).

'Right, I'm not having that!' stormed George. 'It's broad daylight and we're in a public place.' George pushed himself back from the window and stepped towards the doorway. He opened the shop door slowly; there was no bell or buzzer and the two people at the counter were so wrapped up in each other that they didn't notice that anyone had come in.

The old Scotsman was still holding onto his bunch of the flowers tightly, as the little lady ruffled her fingers through his ginger moustache.

'Who's my widdle cuddly wion then? My snuggly wuggly wittle wion.' The lady's voice was sweeter than a sugar cube dipped in honey, and George heard Kenny yak behind him but this sickeningly tender moment had ripped the fury out of his heart.

George and Allison both stopped, neither of the two of them wishing to intrude; George's short-lived anger had now turned to awkward embarrassment. But Crayon Kenny wasn't embarrassed. For the boy who once tried to balance as many £1 coins up his nose as possible was not worried about what people thought of him. He pushed passed George and Allison, who stood there open-mouthed as he declared...

'Can I buy a dead wasp, please?'

The pet-shop lady jumped, wakening from her love-struck dream and she pulled her eyes away from Grandpa Jock. 'No, sorry. We don't sell wasps, young man,' she replied.

'But you've got three in the window,' giggled Kenny, laughing at his own, pathetic joke. Grandpa Jock glanced across.

'George!' he exclaimed. 'About time too, laddie. Elsie, this is my grandson George. George, meet Elsie, my new... er... friend.'

'Ooh yes, young man, your grandfather has been telling me all about you,' she sang in a syrupy voice. Her eyes twinkled as she smiled.

'Pleased to meet you,' nodded George with a grin. He couldn't help himself; the pet-shop lady was lovely. 'And these are my friends, Allison and Cr... er, Kenny, just Kenny.'

'You don't happen to sell any sweets in here, do you?' asked Kenny, pushing forward brazenly; he didn't want the day to be a total disaster.

'No, not really. I'm afraid all I have are these doggy chews,' she replied, and Kenny's eyes lit up again.

'No, Kenny!' Allison said firmly, and Kenny visibly deflated in front of them. The old lady shuffled off to the back of the shop, with promises to find something interesting but Kenny knew it wasn't even going to be a bag of Liquorice Allsorts.

'Well,' buzzed Grandpa Jock eagerly. 'What do you think of her then?'

'She's er… lovely,' grunted George, not quite sure what else to say.

'Oh yes, you can say that again, lad.' Grandpa Jock grinned wildly, glancing across at Elsie searching around the back of her shop. 'I'm taking her out to dinner tonight. It's gonna be really romantic.'

Grandpa Jock was too busy staring at the sweet old shop-keeper as she returned that he didn't notice George and Kenny rolling their eyes together. He didn't even mind when she bustled the children towards the door; he was lost in his little Elsie world.

'Now I just need to chat to your grandpa about tonight,' she sang. 'So you three run along and take good care of these pets for me.' And she handed George, Kenny and Allison a bag each and ushered them out the door.

In the street they all looked at their own bag nervously. Allison held up a clear plastic sack filled with water. Inside the bag was a tiny little goldfish swimming backwards and forwards.

'Cute!' squealed Allison. 'I've always wanted to one of these. What did you get, George?'

George opened the brown paper bag a bit further. He shook it about, trying to see what was at the bottom.

'I think it's a twig?' moaned George.

'Why would the old lady give you a twig, George? She trusted Allison with a goldish.'

George poked around in the bag, certain there was

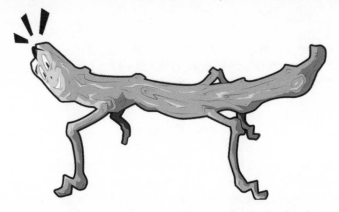

nothing else in there, until a long, spindly leg poked out from the corner. Then another, and another, and another, and another.

'Hang on, it's a stick insect!' cried George. 'Cool!'

'Two stick insects,' yelled Kenny. 'I've got two stick insects in my bag!'

'Wait, so have I,' George shouted. 'There's another one hiding in here.'

'Maybe they're both couples, you know, married. And Elsie's given us them to look after, when they have lots of sticky babies.'

'Sticky babies?' squeaked Allison. 'I don't think stick insect offspring are called sticky babies.'

'What are they called then? Baby twigs?' George laughed but a thought spread slowly across Kenny's face and his mouth dropped downwards.

'Wait, I can't take these. My mum would go mental,' said Kenny sadly. 'She hates bugs, and with Johnny being sick all day she's not going to be in the best of moods. George, can you look after Sticky and Twiggy for me, at least until I can persuade my mum?'

'Sticky and Twiggy?' Allison shook her head. 'Is that the most original names you can come up with for your new pets?'

'Well, what are you calling your fish? Goldie?'

'No, Jaws,' replied Allison, quite sure no one had ever thought of an awesome name like that for a goldfish before.

Last Chapter

They all wandered back slowly to Kenny's house and George had happily agreed to look after his two pets for a few days. He placed Kenny's two stick insects into the other bag so they'd be one big happy family but Kenny was still hopeful he could talk his mum round. 'I'll get them later,' he insisted. 'Maybe in a day or two.'

Allison headed home for her lunch with 'Jaws' the tiny fish, in its little bag, and George walked round to his Grandpa Jock's house. Grandpa Jock had the best video games his old age pension money could buy, even games that George's mum would be shocked to know he played.

'Just shut your ears,' Grandpa Jock would always say, and George spent the afternoon blasting zombies, and hacking, slashing and shooting his way through numerous computer generated battlefields until his thumbs ached and eyes felt as if they were bleeding.

It was late when he switched the console off and went downstairs; hunger driving him in search of food in Grandpa Jock's kitchen but George was surprised when the old Scotsman staggered through the back door, looking as pale as his pants; no wait, George wasn't wearing his white pants today, he had the ones with the little rockets on them but Grandpa Jock was still really ill.

'What's the matter, Grandpa? You look terrible.'

'It was a dreadful night, lad,' he gasped, holding onto the kitchen table.

'Come on, come through and sit down before you fall

down.' And George helped his grandpa into the living room, he flopped down onto the sofa and he puffed hard. George had to turn his head away; Grandpa Jock's breath was stinking!

'I've been sick, George. An upset tummy, or something but it totally ruined the night. I don't think Elsie will want to see me again.'

'I'm sure it's not that bad,' said George, sympathetically. 'She seemed like a really nice lady.'

'Yeah, she is, and the evening started off well,' nodded Grandpa Jock. 'We were in a lovely restaurant, we were both dressed up, she looked gorgeous, George, in a beautiful yellow dress but after we'd eaten our starters I began to feel queasy. It came over me really suddenly, I couldn't help myself.'

'So, you were sick?' asked George, hoping the answer wouldn't be as bad as he was imagining.

'Yeah, right there at the table,' replied Grandpa Jock. George winced. This was going to get worse. Reader, if you are a delicate little person, stop reading now. Just trust me, okay.

'It went all over table, George.' Grandpa Jock closed his eyes, not really sure if he wanted to remember the next bit. 'It went over the plates, it went over the tablecloth, it went over the wine glasses. Projectile vomit splattered all over the restaurant but it gets worse, lad.'

Grandpa Jock went on, 'It went over Elsie!'

'You barfed on your girlfriend?' George couldn't stop himself, the words just blurted out. Grandpa Jock nodded.

'And the worst bit was I had prawn cocktail to start with and a glass of red wine. I was trying to be sophisticated. It was over her dress, red spew splatters covered her yellow frock. Aw man, it covered her head. Little pukey prawns were hiding in her hair, and bits of soggy lettuce stuck to her face, George.'

George thought he was going to sick too (I told you to stop reading) but he held himself together. The two of them sat in silence for a couple of minutes while Grandpa Jock settled down.

'Well, there is a bug going about,' suggested George. 'Kenny's little brother's been sick, or maybe it was something you'd eaten. What did you have to eat this morning?'

'Just toast for breakfast, and a cup of tea as usual.' Grandpa Jock turned his head up to the ceiling as he thought. 'I didn't have anything for lunch but I nibbled on that bag of Twiglets in the kitchen when I came home this afternoon.'

'What bag of Twiglets in the kitchen?' George's eyes widened.

'You know, those knobbly, little snacks. They taste beefy and they look like twigs. There was a paper bag with a few left. I thought you didn't want them.'

'I didn't have any Twiglets this afternoon, Grandpa.'

'I'm not surprised, George. They tasted funny, not very beefy and a bit too crunchy.'

The colour drained from George's face, and it was his turn to feel sick again. He stood up and took a couple of steps towards the toilet before glancing back at Grandpa Jock on the sofa. His cheeks puffed out and he put his hand over his mouth at the watery part. The last thing he managed to shout out was...

'STICK INSECTS!'

And luckily, Grandpa Jock had no idea what he meant.

The End

CENTRIFUGAL FORCE!

When Did the Grass Turn Green?
By Stuart Reid

Granny's house was mouldy and dusty.
Granny's things were old and musty.
Granny's cupboards were crammed with stuff.
Covered with dust and bits of fluff.

Stacks of books and smelly old shoes.
Toy sheep, cows and kangaroos.
Bracelets and bobbles, arts and crafts,
A suitcase filled with old photographs.

'Granny!' shouted George, waving his hand.
'I've found a box from a strange kind of land!'
'Look at these people? Who is this kid?'
He ran with the suitcase and stopped with a skid.

Granny turned and nodded, and said with a smile.
'That's a photograph of me, when I was a child.'
'Wow! Gran, you're ancient! Was it taken long ago?'
'Please tell me everything. I really need to know.'

'What's that? And who's this? Can you show me more?'
Granny smiled patiently, and sat down on the floor.
Thirty minutes passed, an hour, and then two.
Granny slowly stood up, to do what grannies need to do.

'Thanks, Gran,' said George. 'the world has rearranged.'
'I see how houses, cars and clothes have absolutely
changed.'

'But I'm puzzled,' said George, 'by one thing I've seen.'
'When, in the world, did the grass turn green?'

'Your hair's grey in the photos, and it's still grey now.'
'Grass was grey then, but today it's green. How?'
Granny stopped and giggled. 'George, I really need to go.'
'Ask your grandpa, he'll like that. I'm sure that he'll know.'

Out in the garden, Granny thought he was weeding,
George found his grandpa, in his deckchair, quietly
reading.
'Grandpa,' whispered George, 'Can you help? I'm
really keen,'
'To find out when, and how, all the grass turned green?'

George showed him a photo and Grandpa
laughed too.
'The secret,' winked Grandpa, 'is how the sky
turned blue.'
'Grey grass, dull sky. Long ago was never sunny.'
'I mentioned that to Granny but she just thought it
was funny.'

Grandpa teased, 'I blame Henry.
It was his fault way back...'
'He made cars in different colours,
as long as they were black.'

'Now, run along. Go ask your dad, if you want to learn
some more.'
But before George could turn around, Grandpa began
to snore.

Grandpa was right; the world had changed...
long ago, things were duller.
And Mum says dads knows everything.
He'll know who added colour!

George found Dad in the garage, tinkering with his car.
Dad looked up and quietly said, 'What's wrong, my
little star?'

'I'm so confused,' wailed poor George.
'The world's a total mystery!'
'When was colour added, Dad?
Who updated history?'

But Dad just laughed, and laughed, and laughed. 'You're
funny, little chum.'
'Run into the house,' Dad chuckled. 'Go and ask
your mum.'

'MUM!' yelled George at the top of his voice. 'Why's everyone so mean?'
'No one's saying how the sky turned blue, or when the grass turned green!'

Mum hugged George, and went to fetch,
An album from the room.
She took out all the photos.
'Now let me lift the gloom.'

The pictures were bright and colourful;
Grass was green, and sky was blue.
'That's me and dad when our world changed.
That little baby's you!'

'Your grandpa and your dad are teasing,' said Mum softly, without scorn.
'The whole world began to glitter, on the day that you were born.'
'It's the same for all the children, who are loved as much as you.'
'Life just becomes more colourful, every shade and tint and hue.'

At last George knew the truth. He thought,
'I was born with extra sprinkles!'
'But just one thing, Mum,' wondered George,
'Who added all your wrinkles?'

The End